Duck Stays in the Truck

For Sam, Dean, and Cassiel
—D. C.

To baby Briar, the latest addition
to the Lewin clan
—B. L.

SIMON SPOTLIGHT
An imprint of Simon & Schuster Children's Publishing Division
1230 Avenue of the Americas, New York, New York 10020
This Simon Spotlight edition May 2020
Text copyright © 2020 by Doreen Cronin
Illustrations copyright © 2020 by Betsy Lewin
All rights reserved, including the right of reproduction in whole or in part in any form.
SIMON SPOTLIGHT, READY-TO-READ, and colophon are registered trademarks of Simon & Schuster, Inc.
For information about special discounts for bulk purchases, please contact Simon & Schuster Special
Sales at 1-866-506-1949 or business@simonandschuster.com.
Manufactured in the United States of America 0322 LAK
10 9 8 7 6 5 4 3 2
Library of Congress Cataloging-in-Publication Data
Names: Cronin, Doreen, author. I Lewin, Betsy, illustrator.
Title: Duck stays in the truck / by Doreen Cronin ; illustrated by Betsy Lewin
Description: Simon Spotlight edition. I New York, NY : Simon Spotlight, 2020. I Series: A click, clack book I
Audience: Ages 5 - 7. I Summary: "Farmer Brown wants to go camping. He packs up the animals. He
packs up his brother, Bob. The chickens want to hike. The cows want to fish. The pigs want to picnic.
And Duck? Duck just wants to stay in the truck. How will Farmer Brown bring everyone together?"
—Provided by publisher.
Identifiers: LCCN 2019041525 I ISBN 9781534454149 (paperback) I ISBN 9781534454156 (hardcover) I
ISBN 9781534454163 (ebook)
Subjects: CYAC: Camping—Fiction. I Domestic animals—Fiction. I Farmers—Fiction.
Classification: LCC PZ7.C88135 Dw 2020 I DDC [E]—dc23
LC record available at https://lccn.loc.gov/2019041525

A Click Clack Book

Duck
Stays in the Truck

By Doreen Cronin

Illustrated by Betsy Lewin

Ready-to-Read

Simon Spotlight

New York   London   Toronto   Sydney   New Delhi

Farmer Brown is going camping.
He packs the animals.
He packs a tent.
He packs his brother, Bob.

"We are going to Breezy Lake!"
says Farmer Brown.

"We can hike together!

We can fish together!

We can picnic together
in the shade!"

Bob sits in the front seat
with Farmer Brown.
"I have the map," says Bob.
"I will show you the way
to Breezy Lake!"

Bob looks at the map.
"Go this way," says Bob.

Farmer Brown goes this way.

Bob looks
at the map.

"Go that way," says Bob.
Farmer Brown goes that way.

Bob looks at the map.
"We are here!"
says Bob.

"This is not Breezy Lake!"
says Farmer Brown.
"This is the library!"

"We need books to go camping!"
says Bob.

Everyone picks out a book
from the library.

Bob and the animals
pile back in the truck.

Bob sits in the back this time.
Duck sits up front with the map.
"Show me the way to Breezy Lake!"
says Farmer Brown.

Duck looks at the map.
Duck points this way.
Farmer Brown turns this way.
Duck looks at the map.
Duck points that way.
Farmer Brown turns that way.

Duck looks at the map.
The cows point straight ahead.
Farmer Brown drives straight ahead.

The sign says "Welcome to Breezy Lake!"

"We are here at Breezy Lake!"
says Farmer Brown.
"We can hike together!
We can fish together.
We can picnic together
in the shade!"

The chickens turn left.
They head up the mountain.
Chickens love to hike!

Duck stays in the truck.

The pigs turn right.
They find the perfect spot
in the shade.
Pigs love to picnic!

Duck stays in the truck.

The cows walk straight ahead.
They bring their fishing poles.

Cows love to fish!

Duck stays in the truck.

Farmer Brown and Bob
set up the tent.

"We are at Breezy Lake,"
says Farmer Brown.
"But we are not together!"

Bob lights a campfire.

Bob gathers long sticks.

Bob unpacks the marshmallows.

The chickens see the campfire
and return from their hike.
The pigs see the campfire
and return from their picnic.
The cows see the campfire
and return from fishing.

Duck gets out of the truck.

Farmer Brown is happy.
"We can sit together!
We can read together!

We can toast marshmallows together!"

It is a good day at Breezy Lake.